WITCHES

AND

LEGENDS

TWO

Episodes
Five thru Eight

by J. Smith Kirkland

Introduction

Witches And Legends is a tale about modern day witches derived from legends and told in soap opera format. *Witches And Legends* is composed of sixteen episodes, published in four paperback books.

Two: "Curses And Cures" touches on two legends. One brings a visitor from an ancient legend to visit the world of the local witches. And he brings vengeance with him. Aron finds himself needing the witches' help again, and Jack finds the witches need his help this time. The second story finds another stranger in town. She has more than one purpose for coming here, but the players in this book seem to attract those who deal in revenge. She has her eye on Aron, and she is not one to be denied what she wants.

Table of Contents

Episode Five

STONE COLD

No More Magic

Jack has been working up the nerve to tell Selanya that he doesn't want to study magic any longer. He's not sure why he is hesitant to tell her. It's not like it was her idea in the first place. This whole witch world he fell into is just more than he wants to deal with. His brother is back from whatever dark wonderland he was lost in, and now Jack just wants to put all that behind him. He is grateful to Selanya and the others for helping him find his brother. He just hopes Selanya understands.

"Now that Aron's back, I just think . . . all the magic stuff. You know?"

"I understand completely, Jack."

Jack continues explaining, "Aron seems to be doing fine. Jenna is still mad."

"Yeah, I don't think I'll get an invitation to the wedding."

"That's a good bet, "Jack agrees, "She still doesn't believe in witches. She thinks Aron had an accident and has amnesia. He still can't remember the missing days very well."

"What does Aron think?"

"I'm not sure he believes me either, but he does know something weird happened. He's having nightmares. I think memories are starting to come back to him in little flashes. And now that I think about it, he was acting sorta weird today, spaced out a few times."

Selanya wants to believe no bad effects remain from Sunder's mishandled spell. Aron seems ok, but she knows spells like that have a way of clutching onto a person and causing unexpected repercussions.

"You should keep an eye on him for a while."

"I go over when Jenna's not there."

Even though the relationship had only been student and apprentice, this sort of feels like a breakup to Jack. And one of those where she is going to get over it faster than he does. But he has to get back to the real world.

"Look. Thanks for everything. No more magic for me, but we can stay in touch, right?"

"That'll be good. You should stop by again soon. We don't have to do any witchcraft."

She gives him a hug. And a smile to let him know everything is ok between them.

"Bye, Jack."

"Bye, Selanya."

Wedding Plans

Jenna and Aron have started planning their wedding again. Jenna wanted to wait until they were confident Aron was completely recovered, but he assures her he is fine. He wants her to be happy, and planning the wedding makes her happy. She is trying not to stray too far from the original plans.

"I can get the garden on in three months, and the same caterer can do it then, but I'll have to get a different band."

"What about that band your cousin likes? Red Sun?"

She answers as she keeps sorting through a stack of flyers and papers with notes she has been keeping. "Son Red. Yeah, I thought about that. Or Moses Mayfield. Are they still together?"

Aron offers a suggestion, "Maybe Jack could play acoustic?"

She stops sorting and flashes an angry look at him before returning immediately to her task. It's fast, but Aron does not miss it.

"Jack is only going to be there because he's your brother. The less I know he's there the better."

"You know he was just as worried about me. And something weird did happen."

This time the angry look lasts longer than a moment.

"Just stop. Things are getting back to normal. Finally. No more witch tales before my wedding. Or after."

She says more, but Aron spaces out for a moment. When Aron comes back from wherever his mind wondered, she is concluding her thoughts on the subject.

"After the wedding, I'll forgive him, and maybe figure out how to help him get that stuff out of his head too."

"Hey honey, I forgot to get something at the store earlier. I'll be back in a few minutes. You need anything?"

"I can't think of anything. I'm going to meet the caterer in a little while. I may not be here when you get back. Oh. But you know, while you're out, get something for dessert. I've been having a weird craving for sweets."

Stone

The bell over the door doesn't ring as a man enters the shop, but Selayna notices him right away. He strides in wearing a long coat, boots, jeans, and a shirt with leather laces at the neck. He walks with confidence towards the counter and flashes a smile that almost makes her forget how to speak. But being the good shopkeeper that she is, she manages her usual greeting.

"Good morning. Can I help you find anything today?"

"Hi. I'm new to town. Just finding my way around. Checking out all the local shops."

"Welcome to town. Where are you from?"

"All over. But I used to live here. Been away a long time. How long have you been here?"

"I was born nearby. Seems like I've been here forever."

He tilts his head and smiles.

"You look very familiar."

"I hear that I look familiar a lot. My family has been living in the hills around here for a long time.."

He moves a little closer and shares an impish grin.

“These hills are beautiful, aren't they? Like their people.”

He flashes that disarming smile again. Selanya feels a blush steal across her cheeks.

“It's nice to be back. My name is Stone.”

“It's nice to have you back. Selanya.”

Stone picks up the book on the counter in front of Selanya. He leans casually on the counter as he thumbs through it.

“You're reading a book on herbs? I'm somewhat of an expert on medicinal herbs myself,” Stone says.

“Really? An expert?”

She is always suspicious that anyone who has to tell you they are an expert probably isn't. But she is willing to play along in this case. She notices a pendant around his neck. A simple sandstone carved with abstract lines.

“That's a very nice stone.”

He looks down as if he had forgotten he was wearing it and remarks, “Old family heirloom.”

“It's beautiful.”

He flashes his mischievous smile at her. “I like being surrounded by beautiful things.”

She smiles back, “Don't we all?”

Stone's smile widens. “I have to go, but I promise to stop by again. I'll bring you some of my herbal recipes to look at.”

“I'll be looking forward to it.”

Selanya watches him through the window as he walks

away. She turns to find Shamus beside her, not entirely unexpected, but displaying a very disapproving look.

"Now what have I done?" she asks.

Brothers

Aron tries to focus on the surroundings, but even as they become less blurry, they are not familiar. Great. Another alley. Then he sees the blood on his shirt. And his hands. He can't see the blood on his face. He looks around. No one else in the alley. He walks out to the road and gets his bearings. Downtown. He knows this street. Now if he can get home without being seen.

He manages to avoid passing anyone too closely all the way to the house. He quietly opens the back door.

"Jenna? You here?"

No answer. He goes to the laundry room and throws his clothes in the washer, washes the blood from his hands and face, then heads to the bedroom to get fresh clothes. Ones without blood. He is trying not to think about it. Just as he is putting on a clean shirt, he hears the back door open. It's Jack.

"Aron, you home?"

As far as Jack can tell, Aron seems to be mostly back to normal. A little spacey, but Jack rationalizes that's somewhat normal for Aron. Jack hasn't been pushing him much. He thinks Aron needs to build his strength back. So Jack has been patiently hanging out with him while Jenna is at work, but it's time to ask what all Aron remembers.

Aron finds Jack in the kitchen. They exchange their usual brotherly greetings.

"Hey."

"Hey."

Then Jack gets straight to the reason he came over.

"Have you remembered anything else?"

Aron avoids looking directly at Jack.

"Just the stuff from the dreams."

"The ones where someone is chasing you?"

Aron pauses, then answers like he is correcting someone's grammar.

"Some-*thing*."

"Yeah."

Then Aron fills in some new details that he has not given Jack before.

"I remember you chasing me too, but it wasn't you."

"If it wasn't me, who was it?"

Aron corrects him again, "*What* was it."

"Right. And it *was* me chasing you through the alleys. I still don't know how you got away from me."

"Probably because you can't run," Aron taunts.

"*You* can't run," Jack taunts back.

"Yeah, well you couldn't catch me, old man."

Jack laughs.

“It's nice to have you back, little bro.”

“Yeah, well before you get all mushy, Jenna is going to be back soon, and she's still upset with you and all the witch talk.”

Aron drops the conversation and stares across the room at nothing in particular.

“I know,” Jack says. “I hope she gets over it soon; I'd never outrun *her* if she came after me. Learned that one time when I said, 'You run like a girl.' Do you think I can do anything to make up for it? The witch thing that is. I think she got over the other comment when she tackled me. Hey, remember when she clobbered both of us in that mega water gun war?”

Jack waits for a response. There is n one.

“You ok?”

“Yeah, no, I was just thinking Jenna will be home soon, and I don't think you should be here. Not till she's had time to cool off a little more.”

“Okay, but if you keep spacing out like that, you're going back to the doctor.”

“Okay, Mother. You're the boss.”

“That's right; don't you forget it.”

A New Friendship

Sunder likes pretty things. Shiny bobbles, particularly gemstones. She is browsing at the jeweler for a new acquisition. As she looks in a mirror, admiring how nice this silver necklace looks on her, she doesn't notice Stone walk up beside her. He smiles at her, but says nothing, which intrigues her. She waits for him to speak, but when it's obvious he's not going to, she finds something to say.

"They have some nice pieces here."

"Yes, I'm finding all sorts of beautiful things today."

His flashes his disarming smile. Does Sunder blush? Surely not. She is usually the one that makes someone else blush. She knows all about flirting, and she knows it when she sees it. She'll play along.

She asks him, "Have you found anything you liked here before?"

"No, I haven't been here before, but I do have my eye on something today," he says without his gaze leaving her eyes, "You remind me of someone I knew once," he continues, "She came here from a place near the Danube River, near Budapest."

"I hear that I look familiar a lot, but never like someone from Budapest."

He moves a little closer and shares an impish grin.

"You should visit. Budapest is beautiful, like the people there."

A line that apparently gets used a lot, and again that disarming smile. If she were not already in a relationship, she would enjoy this little game, but she has Jack. Not that Jack knows it yet, but he will.

“Look, I'm flattered, but I'm committed to someone.”

That was a good way to word it. Not in a committed relationship with him, just committed to him.

“Of course. I'm sorry. I didn't mean to pour it on that strong. I'm new in town, and don't know anyone. I could use some interesting people to talk to. Can we start over?”

Sunder pretends to think about it for a moment before responding.

“I guess so. I know what it's like to try to meet new people.”

Stone smiles, “Tell you what, I have a reservation for dinner this evening just down the street. Join me? Completely platonic.”

Sunder doesn't usually dine with people that she doesn't know much about, or that she hasn't researched in detail and doesn't know exactly how associating with them can benefit her.

“Well,” she starts, about to decline, but he interrupts.

“I really need conversation with someone besides my cat.”

A man with a cat. An interesting man with a cat. An interesting, handsome man. For a moment she forgets her 'commitment' to Jack.

"You have a cat?"

"More like the cat has me."

She doesn't know what about him is so intriguing. She wonders if he really has a cat. She doubts it, but she finds herself wanting to know more about this new stranger in town.

"Well, okay. To save you from talking to your cat all the time. I suppose I have to eat anyway."

"Good. I have to eat sometimes too. I think you and I may have a lot in common."

Has He Met Your Parents?

Shamus stares at Selanya like a parent at a misbehaving child.

"I haven't done anything," she protests.

Shamus raises an eyebrow but says nothing.

She continues her defence, "His brother is back, and Jack is giving up his magic lessons. Honestly, Shamus, I am not even trying to figure out why the whole thing happened."

"Word on the street is you are playing with fire again."

"I don't know what you're talking about. And who are you talking to on the streets?"

Shamus raises his chin smugly, "I'd rather not say, but they tell me you've been hanging around with a bad element."

“I still don't know what you're talking about, Shamus. This is why Jack calls you the crypto man.”

Shamus feigns hurt at the name calling, but actually approves of the moniker. The crypto man. Drop the article and it has a superhero feel. Crypto Man. But he returns his focus to Selanya, “Flirting with disaster?”

“Are you talking about the guy that was just in here?”

“Ah, so you do know what I mean.”

Selanya smiles, “He seemed rather nice. And interested in herbal medicines.”

Shamus adds, “And rather good looking?”

“Listen young man, you're entering into territory that's none of your business.”

Shamus asks her, “What do you know about him?”

She is about to repeat the “none of your business” argument when she realizes these maybe not-so-fictional people on the street really have told Shamus something. Maybe something she should know.

“Obviously, Shamus, the question is what do you know about him?”

Laundry

Jenna comes into the laundry room to find Aron moving clothes from the washer to the dryer.

"What are you doing?"

Aron turns quickly and throws the shirt in his hand into the dryer behind him.

"Just needed to do a little laundry. I can do laundry."

"I'm not complaining, just surprised. Pleasantly surprised. Do you think the bump on the head has something to do with this new skill of yours? A laundry savant?"

Aron goes back to moving the clothes. He doesn't banter back as he usually would.

"This is not the first time I've done laundry."

"I was just kidding."

He throws the last piece in the dryer and starts it tumbling.

"I'm sorry, Jenna. I'm just tired. After I get these out of the dryer, I think I'll go to bed."

Jenna realizes he's too tired or too something to be playful. And not that she minds, but him doing laundry borders suspicious activity.

"Are you ok?"

"I'm fine, just tired."

"Why don't you go on up to bed, and I'll finish the laundry," she offers

“Ok. Thanks. I'm sorry.”

He gives her a kiss and heads towards the bedroom. She looks around the kitchen for the dessert, but there is none. He must not be feeling well if he forgot to get a dessert. Later, when she gets the clothes from the dryer, she noticed a stain on his shirt that didn't wash out. She looks at it but is not sure what kind of stain it is. Still, he was hiding it for some reason. Why would he try to hide a stain on his shirt?

The Background Check

“You're telling me that you think this guy is a witch?” Selanya asks.

Shamus answers her with furrowed brow and tightened lips.

“Well, I still think it's nothing that concerns you,” Selanya continues in the face of his silence, “but that could be a good thing, him being a witch.”

Selanya is not sure why Shamus is concerned. She likes the idea that this new guy in town could be a witch. An attractive, personable witch who is into medicinal herbs. She is definitely liking this idea.

“Not exactly,” Shamus responds. “He's more than that. He's older than that. He's older than you. He taught your people about conjuring.”

“My people?”

"You know what I mean: your family. Your ancestors. The ones from here."

She starts to get what Shamaus is saying in his usual riddle-like way, "Taught them? You're saying he's the old one? How can that be? That can't be."

"I don't know. They killed him. Or I thought they killed him. They thought they killed him. Legend writers and witch historians all say they killed him. Everyone thought he was dead. But obviously he's not."

"Shamus, focus."

Shamus looks at her seriously, "He's not dead, obviously."

"Shamus. Are you sure about this?"

"He's the ancient one. The first wizard. The first witch. The first vampire. The first monster under the bed. The first legend that spawned all other legends. Your people called him Stone. They turned him to ash, so the legends say."

"Then how did he come back?"

Shamus ponders her questions, then replies, "Or maybe the question is, why did he come back?"

Enemy of My Enemy

It's the most expensive restaurant in town. Reservations only. Pretentious. Portentous. Sunder loves it.

They are having an excellent meal, talking about the local art and music. Typical "getting to know you" conversation. Then Stone slightly leans in towards her from across the table.

"Look, I'm going to get to the point. I know you're more than people think you are."

Sunder is not sure where this is headed. What could he possibly know about her?

He continues, "I'm more talented than people think, too. I don't need to explain that to you. Do I?"

He doesn't. Somehow, he knows she is a witch. But she is not ready to give herself away completely. She responds simply, "No."

"And I think you and I have something else in common too. A common, well, let's not say enemy. A common adversary."

"What do you mean?"

"Selanya."

Now he has her full attention, "Continue."

"To put it bluntly, her family did me a great injustice, and I want revenge. And she seems to be moving in on your territory. Yes?"

Sunder raises her eyebrows to confirm his hypothesis.

"Well then, Sunder, maybe if the two of us work together, we could both get what we want."

Not Over Yet

Aron wakes up, not sure if it's morning or night. He went to bed too early. But his usually soft bed feels firm and itchy. As he sits up, a leaf crinkles beneath his hands. This is not his bedroom. This is the woods. He looks at the ground around him. His hands have blood on them again. His clothes are torn, muddy. He is on the edge of panicking.

You have to hold it together, he tells himself. Could be a dream.

The wind rustles the leaves in the trees above him. Not a dream. In the woods. Which woods?

He tries to remember something, anything after going to bed. A dream. Running. He remembers a street. There are buildings with galleries, like in the French Quarter. A woman in a blood red dress with a black scarf around her head. And a rabbit running through a field of lavender.

That had to be a dream; there is nothing near here like any of that. But then, he doesn't know where here is. He *hopes* there is nothing like that near here.

His pats the pocket of his jeans to see if his cell phone is there. It is. He takes it out. He is happy to see it has a signal. Maybe he is not too far from home. He makes a call.

"Jack. Help me."

Episode Five

THE WIND

Call The Wind

Stone and Sunder are continuing their conversation as they walk through the park. The table at the restaurant was a bit too exposed to be discussing how to destroy Selanya's powers. Stone knows a lot more about Selanya than Sunder could have imagined.

"The wind is her strength. And her weakness, " He tells Sunder

"The wind?"

"Yes. We can weaken her by casting our spells together onto the wind. Then when she is weak enough, we can take her powers from her. It's not without some risk. She'll know what we're doing."

Sunder has no lack of confidence, and she has seen nothing from Selanya to indicate she has much power at all. She's more of an academic than a real witch.

"How much of a threat can she be?"

Stone leans in to put emphasis on his words.

"You have no idea."

He goes back to his explanation of the plan.

"Tomorrow, what we have to do is hold a blade into the wind as we cast a spell on her, but it has to be strong enough that she can't stop us."

"I'm not afraid of her."

"You should be. As soon as we hold the blade to the wind, she'll know someone is casting a spell. Like I say, the wind is her strength."

I'm Not Crazy

Once Jack reminded Aron there was GPS on his phone, Jack picked him up at a nearby trailhead. He took Aron by his place and gave him some clean clothes before sneaking Aron back into the house. Fortunately, Jenna had not wanted to wake him and was asleep 'watching television' in the living room.

The next morning, as if he had been waiting outside in his car all night, Jack comes in just after Jenna leaves for work. He knew Aron was spacing out, but not that he was blacking out, losing hours of time, and maybe killing something. Or someone.

Aron whispers to Jack, "Did you wash my clothes?"

"She's gone. Why are you whispering? And I burnt them instead."

"What!"

"Just a precaution."

Jack doesn't know if he has become an accomplice to a crime or not, but he has to believe nothing bad really happened. His brother isn't capable of hurting anyone.

"Look, no murders have been on the news, no animal mutilations. For all we know, you fell on something dead in the woods. Your arms are scraped up, so it was probably your own blood. You probably wiped your mouth with your bloody arm. Worst case, you ate a bird or a squirrel or something."

The idea of eating an animal in the woods makes Aron queasy. He isn't going vegetarian like Jenna anytime soon, but he likes his steaks medium well.

"I don't remember anything. I leave to go to the store, or to the kitchen, or to take a nap, and I wake up somewhere else with blood all over me."

Jack, puts his hand on Aron's shoulder, "We're gonna get you some help, Aron. A good doctor. Tell them about the amnesia, and the dreams, but just leave out the part about the blood."

"Do you think I'm crazy?"

"No."

Jack says it with conviction, but inside he is not so sure.

"I don't think you're crazy. I think it was Sunder's spell. Maybe it's making you sleepwalk."

"Then what do you think a doctor will do for me? If she turned me into some kind of Jekyll and Hyde, what's a doctor going to do for me?"

"I don't know."

Aron works up the nerve to say what he knows Jack doesn't want to hear.

"We have to go see your friend. Selanya."

Seven Sisters

Selanya opens a freshly delivered box of new books. She takes a stack of them out and is going to place them on the counter, but her grip is weak. She drops them. She sits down in one of the chairs in the reading area and tries to think what she could have eaten, or not eaten, to make her feel so fatigued. Then the bell over the door clatters with excitement. It's Jack.

He goes straight into the issue as soon as he sees her.

“Selanya, I know I said I'm done, but what can we do for Aron? He's blacking out. He woke up in the woods with blood on his hands.”

Aron follows right behind him.

“I don't want to be a monster.”

Selanya starts to get up, but dizziness forces her to sit back down. Jack realizes he has been concentrating on his problem and hasn't even said hello or notice how pale Selanya looks.

“Are you ok?”

“I'm fine; just need to eat something I guess. Let me see what else I can find out about that potion of Sunder's. Maybe I'll see if I can find the Sweet Woman again. Right now, you two should go home. Don't let Aron out of your sight.”

“Ok, but call me as soon as you know anything.”

"I will ."

Jack watches her as she stands back up. "Or if you need anything. You sure you're ok?"

"Yes. Just low blood sugar, I'm sure."

Jack accepts that explanation. He gets hangry himself at times. He and Aron start for the door. Aron looks back.

"Thanks, Selanya," Aron says.

"No problem."

Selanya sits down and closes her eyes. She hears Shamus next to her, "You don't look well."

Without opening her eyes, she says, "I'll be fine."

"Are you sure?"

"Yes, Shamus. I'll be fine. But Aron has started blacking out. He wakes up somewhere else with blood on his hands."

"You have more to worry about than that right now."

Selanya argues, "He needs help."

"Selanya. I don't know how the Cherokee *destroyed* Stone before, but I'm pretty sure he's out for revenge on the descendants of the individuals that did it."

"That was so long ago; how could he ever trace that lineage?"

"Think about it. It had to have been witches. From this part of the country? From these hills? Some of the legends of how they captured him talk about seven women. Seven sisters. Seven matriarchs. Sound familiar?"

Selanya opens her eyes.

"My grandmother."

Girl Talk

Sunder has invited Jenna to come over on her lunch break. Supporting Jenna while Aron was missing has become a good way to keep tabs on Jack. Sunder is going to continue to play on the new bond between them. She pours Jenna a cup of tea and sits down with her at the table. Sunder's plan is to start with something about Jenna, pretend to care, then slyly move the topic to Jack. But Jenna has her own plan and starts to interrogate Sunder.

"So who is this new guy you've been seen with?"

"Who told you that?"

"Oh, it's a small town. I have my sources."

Sunder is not pleased that Jenna has *sources*. Or that these sources are reporting back about her own movements.

"He's just a friend. Not even that. More of a business acquaintance."

"A good-looking business acquaintance is what I hear. And it was a pretty romantic setting for a business dinner."

Sunder does not like anyone prying into her business, much less Jenna. She prefers to be the one steering the conversations. But this is just the chance to take back control.

"You know my heart belongs to someone else."

"I know. I just think you could do better."

"Jenna, you can't stay mad at Jack forever. You're marrying his brother."

"I'm gonna be mad at him a little longer. But he's done with the magic stuff. He said he was anyway."

Sunder is pleased, "So he won't be hanging around that woman at the bookstore anymore? That's good."

Not Even for a Minute

Jack and Aron are planning to binge Vincent Price movies for the whole afternoon. What goes with black and white thrillers? Popcorn? No, maybe a club sandwich. Jack gets up to go to the kitchen.

"You want a sandwich, Bro?"

"Nah. Jenna is going to bring curry home tonight. I'm saving up for that."

"All right. I'm gonna make one for me."

Jack opens the fridge and studies the contents to see what he can find to tempt his taste buds.

"So what time is she going to be home?"

He waits for an answer, as he sets some lunch meat and jars out on the table. Turkey, cream cheese, and strawberry jam. That's a good start.

Jack keeps talking, "I just figured I'd leave before she gets here, so I won't tick her off."

Still no answer.

“Aron?”

Jack goes back to the living room. Aron is gone. The front door is open.

Jack sighs.

“Not again.”

Blades to the Wind

As soon as Jenna leaves, Sunder goes to an old chest in the bedroom and pulls out an elk-horn-handled hunting knife. A gift from her mother. She never knew why her mother had a hunting knife, or where this one originated, but her mother always kept it under lock and key. So Sunder did also. She figured today was as good a day as any to use it.

Sunder moves to her back porch. With her phone in one hand, holding her knife to the wind with the other, she listens to Stone's instructions and follows them.

Stone is somewhere in the woods, holding his phone and raising a stone axe into the wind. His favorite axe, made by an Elder. It still has the stain of the Elder's blood on it.

“We've weakened her, Sunder, but I'm sure she knows it is me. We need to be physically in the same place to make us stronger. How soon can you meet me?”

“I can leave right now.”

Here We Go Again

Jack comes into the shop. Again. He feels like he is in some kind of time loop.

"Selanya? Selanya, Aron is gone again, and I think it's . . ."

He sees Selanya collapsed on the floor. Books are scattered across the room from a short shelf she took down with her. Jack rushes to her and gently lifts her towards a sitting position.

"Selanya. Wake up."

Her eyes open halfway, and she looks at him, but does not speak. He helps her into a chair.

"What happened? Are you ok?"

"I'm getting weaker. I think it's Stone."

Jack does not know what she means. He asks,"Stone?"

She breathes deeply several times.

"A witch, or something more. He came into my store. My ancestors thought they destroyed him centuries ago, but he's back. And wants revenge. On me."

"Revenge? For what? Nevermind. What can I do?"

"Nothing. Unless you know how to destroy the Wizard Stone Clad."

Jack looks puzzled.

"Stone Clad?"

"That was what they called him."

Jack hums a tune. Selanya looks at him, wondering if he is really here, or if she is dreaming. Why is he humming? Then he starts to speak in a sing-song meter.

"Dark and Light, Spirit, Bone. These things will bind him clad in stone."

Jack seems very pleased with his song. Selanya is too weak to explain her confusion. She musters one word.

"What?"

"A rhyme my MawMaw used to sing to me."

Jack pulls the sing-song rhyme from deep in his synapses. He can almost hear it in his MawMaw's voice and see her smile as he sings it with her.

"Seven spirits in these hills only bend the Stone Clad will. Dark and Light, Spirit, Bone. These things will bind him clad in stone."

Selanya realizes this is not just a child's song. As with most nursery rhymes, there is a history behind it.

"Okay," she says, hoping he can remember the rest. "What were these things?"

Jack thinks hard for a minute, reaching back through time to his MawMaw's kitchen, the smell of warm sugar cookies, and his MawMaw singing.

"Dogwood beads, cattail seeds, snowflake carrots, rabbit weed. Water from the mountain's stream."

He pauses. It takes a lot of effort to travel through time to the rest of the rhyme.

"Oh, I remember. 'Dogwood beads, cattail seeds, snowflake carrots, rabbit weed. Water from the mountain's stream. Sends Stone Clad back into our dreams.' Wow, I can't believe I remember that. MawMaw could be so weird sometimes. But she had the best smile. And gingerbread."

"Jack, that's a spell. A potion."

Jack snaps back from his past to this world where . . .

"MawMaw was not a witch!"

"Probably not a witch, but I'd bet your MawMaw knew a few."

Jack refuses the idea his grandmother was a witch. Somehow, it's ok if she knew some.

"I thought it was just all Jabberwocky talk."

Sunder is intrigued, "I've never heard of anyone that remembered how they destroyed Stone Clad. The legends talked about how the women trapped him, not so much about how they destroyed him, but that may be it. Your grandmother may have known the secret."

Selanya starts to get up from the floor, but she is still too weak.

"Take it easy," Jack tells her, "Just sit there. Let me get you some water."

He grabs a water bottle from behind the counter and brings it to her. He waits for her to drink before he starts talking again.

"You mean how they thought they destroyed him. I mean, he's here. Now. So it may not be as strong of a potion as they thought."

"Right. But if it works for another five or ten centuries, maybe we can figure out a better way before then."

Jack ignores the centuries remark. He is trying not to ask questions when he doesn't want the answers. Stuff like how old is the crypto man, or the Sweet Woman, or Sel. . . nope, not going there. But he knows if they need to make potion from his MawMaw's song, then they need the ingredients.

"Do you have all that stuff to mix up?"

Selanya starts going through the list, more to herself than in response to Jack.

"Wild carrots we can find; that's just Queen Anne's lace. Rabbit tobacco, I don't know if it even grows around here anymore, but it's probably in some woods nearby. Cattails and dogwood berries. No, wrong time of year. But you know who will have them."

It takes him a moment, but he realizes she means the Sweet Woman. He mainly thinks about the petits fours when he thinks of her shop, but he knows she also has a reputation for making potions.

"Okay, so first I have to find the constantly moving sweet shop, and then I have to find someone named Stone."

"Shamus is trying to round up my cousins and find more information on Stone. What worries me is that Shamus said Stone had solicited Sunder to help him. Maybe she's with him. I hope she's okay. The Sweet Woman can help you find her, too.

"Sunder. Here we go again."

Curry

Jenna comes in with carryout curry boxes and her slowly returning optimistic persona.

"It's suppertime."

She puts the boxes on the table and starts getting out plates.

"Aron. Suppertime."

She continues setting the table, then stops and listens to the silence through the house. This has become an all too familiar feeling; something is wrong. Aron is not answering. Aron is gone.

"Aron?"

She walks to the living room door and hesitantly looks in. Her first instinct is to call 911 and tell them he is disoriented and lost, but she hesitates. She thinks about the stained shirt, how out of it he was the night before, and the fact that she still has no idea where he was the whole time he was missing. While she refuses to believe in witches and curses, something has been wrong with Aron since he came back. She's afraid to find out what.

Power

Sunder follows an overgrown path through the woods near the creek. Nature is not her favorite place. She doesn't have many outdoorsy outfits, and definitely no shoes made for this rocky trail. In a small clearing, on a large outcrop of rock, she finds Stone waiting.

"I'm glad you could get here so quickly," he says.

Sunder gets straight to the point, "Do you think she's weak enough to take her powers yet?"

"Almost, but I'm not quite strong enough yet. That's why I needed you, and your powers."

Sunder is filled with adrenaline and excitement at the thought of the two of them taking down Selanya. She holds the knife out in front of her.

"We can combine our powers."

Stone walks over slowly, pulls her wrist down gently so the knife points to the ground. Then he tightens his grasp.

"Yes, but not exactly the way you're thinking."

The Right Stuff

Jack is once again in the sweet shop. This time it looks like a candy store from the 1960s. The walls are lined with shelves of jars holding an assortment of sweets: wax lips, peanut butter bars, cherry sours, Lemon Heads, Double Lollies, Now and Laters. The Sweet Woman looks the same.

He has explained everything he knows to her, and she has been busy creating the odd concoction. She hands him a large jug of liquid.

"Are you sure that was the whole rhyme, Jack?"

Jack is not certain. He knows she knows that.

"I think so."

"For Selanya's sake, I hope you're right. You know how to get there?"

"I think so."

"You think so? Look, I would just send you there myself, but I don't feel like dealing with a lecture from Shamus if he found out. Or worse if you landed wrong. Now, do you know where you're going?"

"Yes."

"Good. The legends are all over the place. You may have to pour it on his ear, maybe his nose. Your guess is as good as mine. Now, how are you going to get close enough to pour that on him at all?"

Jack thinks about that very hard for a minute, then smiles.

Betrayal

Stone has Sunder's hands tied behind her with feet bound, and she is lying face down on the ground. He stands over her with her mother's knife. He is about to drain Sunder of her powers and her blood.

"Stupid fairy witch. I bet you wish you'd never met me. Wish. Oh that's funny. See what I did there? You know what I wish? I wish I had all your life energy to make me stronger. Can you make that wish come true?"

She mumbles something angrily through the sleeve that he ripped off of her shirt to gag her.

"No? Let's see what I can do about that then."

Stone kneels down and feels the blade of Sunder's knife. He runs a finger across the side of her neck. But before he can turn the blade on her, there is a rustling of underbrush, and Jack comes stumbling out of them.

"Get away from her!"

Stone turns to see Jack. He laughs.

"What are you going to do, mortal?"

"This."

Jack pulls out a super-sized, brightly colored, plastic water gun. Stone laughs at him even harder as Jack shoots him with the water gun. But his laughter turns to shock and then anger as he realizes Jack has actually found the potion made by his worse enemy. Stone starts to shake. His irises blacken.

"Oh, now that's only going to tick me off. "

Jack keeps shooting as Stone walks toward him. Jack shoots him once in the ear. Then the forehead. Stone keeps walking. Then Jack hits Stone's hand. Stone drops the knife, jumps back, and grimaces, holding his hand with the other.

Jack smiles. “So that's the spot.”

Stone tries to shield his hands while retrieving the blade. Jack circles him. He shoots Stone's hand repeatedly. Enough potion has hit Stone to keep him from doing anything to stop the attack from continuing. He falls to his knees and shivers dramatically. Jack runs over to Sunder laying on the ground.

“You can't destroy me that easily.” Stone laughs, “That makes me weak for a minute, but this is not over.”

Stone stands up and slowly moves toward Jack. Jack shoots at him, but the gun is out of water.

“I knew I should have bought two of these.”

Stone grabs Jack's forearm, and Jack feels a cold pain move into his fingertips and up his arm to his shoulder. He can't move. But Stone is too weak to do more than that to Jack.

“How did you get her potion? You weakened me, neophyte. But it won't last.”

He throws Jack to the ground. Jack lays frozen, motionless next to Sunder. He is awake, but he is trapped by his own body. His muscles stiffen. His fingertips are turning to stone, and the solidifying sensation is moving up his fingers and into his hands.

“And you don't have what it would take to finish the job, mortal.”

“But I do,” A voice from behind Stone startles him.

Selanya steps out from the woods. Stone smiles. This is too easy. She has come to him.

"You are not as strong as your grandmother, little princess."

Another voice comes from the woods.

"No, but together we are."

Six other women step into the clearing. One picks up the stone hatchet made by the Elder. Betrayed by his own arrogance, Stone carelessly left it laying on the ground as he tied up Sunder. The women slowly surround him. His smile is gone.

Selanya looks him in the eye. "All seven of us. Seem familiar?"

Stone realizes he is too weak to fight them. But he thinks now that they can never destroy him completely.

"You can't defeat me this easily. You're just delaying your fate. Just like before. I will be back. I will have my revenge on you witches. Your human apprentice will pay for this too."

He looks at Jack. Memorizing his face, or perhaps his DNA.

"Don't think you have escaped unharmed, mortal. You're marked now. I will be back for you and yours, and I will eat you alive. If the old hag doesn't get to you first."

The women close their circle around Stone, who falls to the ground. Selanya has her energy back. She sees Jack trying to get up. He falls to his knees, looking at his hands.

She starts to move towards him, but she has a task to finish first.

Jack crawls over to Sunder. He places his cold hand to her forehead. She opens her eyes to see him.

"Jack!"

He starts to untie her. His hands are stiff and clumsy. His fingertips are numb, but he still accomplishes the task. She throws her arms around him.

"You saved me. Even after what I did to Aron."

He doesn't respond. She doesn't know if he won't or can't. But she knows he still loves her.

The women slowly widen the circle. Where Stone stood there is only a pile of thin flat slate, dusted with white ash. The women begin to scatter the ash and slate with their feet, kicking them as they dance in a circle around them and over them.

Jack lies down in the leaves next to Sunder. Selanya walks towards them, carrying the scorched hatchet.

"He still loves me," Sunder whispers deludedly. "Don't you, Jack?"

Jack does not respond. He looks unconscious

Sunder gasps. "Jack!"

Sunder gets to her knees, grabs his shoulders and shakes him. His eyes are still closed, but he starts to move his fingers. Selanya comes over and kneels by him. Sunder pushes her away.

"Stay away from him! What have you done to him?"

"Sunder, Stone did this to Jack, and to you. Are you

okay?"

Selanya gets to her feet and extends her hand to help Sunder stand, but Sunder gets up on her own.

Backing away from Selanya, she threatens, "You'll pay for this."

Aftermath

Selanya takes Jack's arm to help him out of the woods, but Sunder pushes her aside and puts her arm around Jack to steady him as they walk to a trail head parking lot. Six other women are also leaving the woods, dispersing, getting in their cars. Jack's phone rings. He fumbles when answering it, but Sunder helps him. It's Jenna.

"Jack. Have you seen Aron?"

Jack does his best to sound casual and not like he has just been attacked by a monster.

"Aron was at your house when I was there earlier."

Jack looks at Selanya for an answer on what to do.

"I brought dinner home. He was supposed to be here," Jenna tells him.

"Curry, I know, " Jack replies, "It's all he could talk about."

"He's not answering his phone. Jack, I can't take this again."

"Jenna, calm down. I'm on my way."

“I can't go through this again,” she repeats.

“You can't start imagining the worst every time he's late.”

“It's not just that. He's been acting strange lately, and I saw.”

She stops. Jenna hears the back door open.

“Saw what?”

Jenna sighs, “Never mind.”

She tries to steady her voice.

“He's here.”

She ends the call without saying goodbye. Jack looks at Selanya, He doesn't have to say anything. She knows Jack is worried about Aron.

“Aron is back at the house,” he says, “But Jenna knows something is wrong with him.”

He looks at Sunder. The love she is so certain he feels for her is not what she sees in his eyes as he finished his thoughts..

“Something left over from a bad spell.”

Episode Seven

VODOU

For Better or Worse

Aron has come back from his most recent disappearance carrying a grocery bag. Jenna does not want to appear upset. She is angry, scared, not sure what to feel, but she is not going to show it. Even though she has not yet said "for better or worse" in front of witnesses, she is committed to that ideal: for better or worse. There is something wrong with him right now. He needs help, not anger.

"I wondered where you were."

"I realized we didn't have anything to drink with dinner. Bought some Cokes."

He puts the drinks in the refrigerator. Next to the other drinks already there. Then he gives Jenna a hug.

"Sorry I'm late for dinner."

"You're not that late. But we will need to reheat the curry."

As he turns to walk away from her, she notices dirt and a tear in the back of his shirt.

After the Fall

Sunder is ecstatic that Jack has confirmed his true feelings for her. Not in words, but in deed. When Stone was attacking, Jack could have helped Selanya fight him off, but instead he freed Sunder from the ropes Stone had used to bind her. Jack must love her. He must be willing to forgive her for the spell she cast on his brother. It was an accident after all.

“Can I take you home, Jack?”

Jack is still weak from Stone's attack, but he has his voice back now. That's not all good news for Sunder.

“I think you've done enough, Sunder.”

Selanya tries to interrupt before too many words are said in anger. “My car is right here. I think we need to get him home and let him rest.”

Sunder is not going to let Selanya make decisions for Jack. She lashes out at Selanya. “This is all your fault.”

Jack moves close to Sunder's face.

“Are you joking? How is this Selanya's fault? You were the one who made friends with a . . . whatever he was.”

“He was using me, Jack. I didn't know what he was doing. He wanted revenge on . . . *her*. She's the one that brought him here. She's dangerous.”

Selanya takes Jack by the shoulders and eases him away from Sunder. “The two of you can work this out later. Jack is weak. We need to make sure he's okay. You need to rest too, Sunder. One of my cousins can take you home and stay with you if you need.”

Sunder glares at Selanya, then turns wounded kitten eyes back to Jack. “Jack.”

“I'm going with Selanya.”

Sunder does not hide her anger as she turns and walks

away, but she stumbles and grabs a tree to keep from falling.

Selanya motions for one of the women to come help, then speaks soothingly to Sunder.

"Sunder, we need to make sure you're ok, too. Please let them help you."

A couple of the women reach Sunder to support her so she doesn't fall.

"Let me drive you home," one of them says. "Or come home with us and let us fix you some tea."

Sunder gains her composure and pushes them away. "I'm fine. I don't need your help."

But she lets them lead her to their car, because the trees keep circling her, and the ground keeps jumping at the sky.

Tell Me

Aron changed his clothes before dinner. Jenna has not mentioned it. They didn't talk much at all as they ate.

"That was really good, Jenna. Where did you get it?"

"Down on 3rd street. I still like the Thai place better, but this was good."

Aron takes his plate to the sink. A barrage of emotions slam through Jenna's mind as she works up the nerve to ask Aron questions about his odd behavior lately.

"How did you tear that shirt you had on earlier?"

"Did I? I didn't know."

"Is something going on?"

"What do you mean?"

Jenna walks up to him and takes his hand gently.

"You've just been acting a little . . . I don't know . . . distant. I know it must be hard, not remembering what happened to you. You still don't remember anything?"

"I'm sorry, Jenna. I guess it bothers me more than I want to think it does. Not knowing where I was for so long."

"You can talk to me about it, you know."

"I know."

He knows he can't. He knows if he mentions witches or super freaky blackouts, she will snap. He knows he could lose her forever. So he doesn't say any of that stuff.

"I know I can. I just . . . It's weird."

Aron starts to move away. But Jenna stops him.

"I don't just mean about the missing time before. You can talk to me about whatever has been going on since you got back."

"I know."

Aron walks out of the room. All those emotions of anger, fear, and confusion swirl around Jenna as she watches him leave.

The Odds

"I think all of this is more than I can take," Jack says. "Sunder is a witch. You're a witch. Something is freaking weird with Aron."

Selanya has brought Jack to her apartment behind the bookstore. They are sitting in her living room. He didn't want to sleep as she suggested, partly because he was afraid to dream of the real world, then wake up back here. And partly because he was still running on adrenaline from the confrontation with Stone.

"Sorry, Jack. I know you want your regular uneventful life back. But it looks like you have stumbled into our world for some reason."

"Some reason. You mean Sunder. Sunder started all this. And I didn't stumble, she pushed me into this world."

Shamus is suddenly there behind Jack. He is wearing a habit.

"Or maybe you pushed her into this world." Shamus smiles at his own alternative reason.

Jack jumps. "You have to stop doing that."

"Sorry, Jack. Habit."

Selanya sighs at his bad pun.

"Oh, Shamus."

Shamus is wearing his regular clothes now as he walks into Jack's view.

“As I was saying. Maybe you were always supposed to be in this *world*, Jack. Maybe the universe used Sunder to get you here.”

“What does that mean? Why would the *universe* want *me* in this mess?”

“We all have something to offer. To the universe, God, the cosmos, whatever it chooses for you to call it.”

Selanya interrupts Shamus's musings, “That's all great stuff to talk about . . . later, Shamus. Is Jack okay right now?”

“He's fine.”

“But he was really weak when we were in the woods. At first, I wasn't sure he was going to wake up.”

“He's fine. Maybe even better.”

Jack scoffs, exasperated. “Better?”

“What did you feel when Stone touched you?”

“Paralyzed.”

“Is that all?”

Jack thinks about it. No, that wasn't all. He remembers an odd feeling.

“And sorta calm,” Jack adds.

“You felt calm, and what did you think? Remember.”

Jack takes a deep breath and tries to remember. He looks at Selanya with something that seems to her like a cross of understanding and fear.

“That I knew who he was. I knew what he was, and what he could teach me.”

Selanya steps in front of Shamus. She only confronts him with demands when absolutely needed, but she has a feeling it is about to be needed.

“What's going on, Shamus?”

“Jack was touched by the Stone Clad healer. The person that taught your people healing, among other things that we would all rather forget. He wasn't always the bad guy. He could have used his knowledge to destroy Jack, but not without also giving a little bit of it to Jack.”

Jack stands up.

“What does that mean? What did he do to me?”

“Don't know exactly. But it's probably a good thing.”

“*Probably* good? Good for who? Someone like you? Or a mortal like me?”

“Ninety percent chance it's a good thing. For you.”

Jack looks at Selanya with a raised eyebrow.

“Yeah, that makes me feel much better.”

He sits back down and asks Shamus, “So no lasting bad effects?”

“No, none.”

Jack looks at Selanya again. “How accurate is he usually?”

Shamus, still calculating in his head, says, “Eighty percent chance there's none.”

“Wait. It just went down ten percent?”

Jack turns back to Shamus, but he's gone.

Jack shakes his head, “He has got to stop doing that.”

Marinette

“It has to be here somewhere.”

Sunder tosses through the contents of storage boxes in her attic. She cuts her finger on a box edge, makes a noise more of anger than pain, and continues looking. At last, she finds a box containing three Vodou dolls.

“There you are.”

She carefully picks up the Vodou doll wrapped with red and black material and a desiccated sprig of lavender.

“If I remember Mother's stories right, you're the one that can help.”

She closes the box with the other two dolls still inside. As she does she almost drops the lavender-stuffed doll. She gets some of the blood from her cut on it.

“Sorry, Marinette. I'll clean that up later. Right now, we have some work to do.”She carries the doll downstairs to the kitchen.

“I know Jack loves me. He's just upset right now. You have to help make him forgive me. My dear Marinette, what will we do? I guess we should start with a little bonfire.”

Sunder places the doll carefully next to a small black kettle on the stove, then strikes a match.

Some Kind of Vodou

A long table with twelve chairs, set with a decadent array of sweets and savories. Bright plates filled with petit fours, lemon squares, brownies, blondies, sweet potato pound cake muffins, finger sandwiches, and other delicious treats. This feast is set not in a room, or an opening in a forest floor, but in a void. A whiteness that seems to neither begin or end anywhere. There is no horizon, nothing to define the edges. And no other objects in the distance, or nearby, just the table and chairs.

Two people sit at the table, one on each end. The Sweet Woman is leaning back in her chair, eating a white chocolate raspberry bonbon. Shamus sits at his best posture as he enjoys miniature lemon pies.

Hesitating as he reaches for another pie, Shamus looks around the space.

"Did you feel that?"

"What?"

"It was like a tremor. Just a little one."

"You're imagining things, Shamus. It would take some kind of Vodou to cause a tremor here."

"That's exactly what I was thinking."

§

Back in the mortal world, Jenna is on her break and sitting

at a lunch counter enjoying a grilled cheese, crinkle fries, and a Coke. She and the other patrons don't notice as their drink agitate so slightly from the same disturbance Shamus felt.

The others do notice a beautiful, dark, full-figured woman as she walks up to Jenna. She is wearing a red dress with a black scarf, belt, and a necklace of large onyx beads. Her presence demands notice and respect.

“Excuse me. I've just arrived in town, and I was hoping you could help me find where I need to be.”

Out of Cokes

Jack had a decent night's rest, so he has come by to check on his little brother. Jenna was worried enough about Aron that she actually put down her anger long enough to call Jack. She told Jack that Aron couldn't explain why it took him so long just to run to the store for drinks.

“Where did you go yesterday, little brother? You sorta disappeared for a while.”

“The store. We were out of Cokes.”

“You can pull that with Jenna, but you know I know better.”

“I don't know where I went. Or why I went. But when I ended up downtown, I went to the store. I bought Cokes.”

Jack is not buying it. Aron is ready to change the subject.

"And what happened to *you* yesterday, Jack?"

"You don't wanna know. I went Selanya's to get her help finding you, and then witchy crazy happened."

"Sorry."

"Hey, it's not your fault. It's Sunder's."

Jack stops himself from going into details. He is here because his brother needs help. And as much as he hates to admit it, that probably means even more witchy crazy stuff is gonna happen.

"Selanya wants to talk to you. She's hoping we can figure something out. Maybe help you remember where you go."

Aron thinks about the blood on his hands.

"I'm not sure I want to know."

Encounter at the Counter

Jenna asked the woman to join her at the lunch counter. They start talking about local events and places of interest. Jenna likes her. She is so normal. A very elegant normal, but normal. And she's the first person Jenna has talked to in a while about something other than all the drama that's been happening.

"I like living here. There's so much to do downtown or close by. Hiking, climbing, the river, art festivals, music."

"I love finding local art when I visit places," the woman

says.

“Well, there's lots of great shops on Main Street and the North Shore strip.”

“I'll have to check some of them out.”

Jenna remembers an event happening tonight, “There's a gallery, an artist co-op right on the strip. Everything is local. Actually, one of my friends is having his opening there tonight. We're going about seven. You should come.”

“We?”

“My fiancé and I.”

“Is he an artist?”

“No, he's a musician. That's sort of an artist, I guess. You should come tonight and you can meet him.”

“I may just do that. Is there other local art nearby?”

“There's a bookstore. It's mainly books, but it has different things by local artists.”

Jenna wishes she had not said that. She is still angry at Jack and Selanya, but her true caring persona is gradually breaking through the wall she has tried to construct around it. And it is a great shop.

“But?”

The woman calls out Jenna's hesitation.

“I'm just not fond of the woman that works there. But I shouldn't have said that. They have nice things. You might like it.”

“Well, thank you. I hope to see you at the gallery later.”

“I hope so. I've really enjoyed talking to you. I feel like

we've known each other forever. And I'm sorry, I didn't even get your name."

"Marinette, but please call me Mari."

"Marinette. What a beautiful name. It was nice meeting you, Mari."

"And so nice to meet you, Jenna. I look forward to meeting Aron"

Marinette lays some money on the counter. The woman behind the counter comes to take the money, and leaves Jenna's ticket.

Jenna thinks out loud, "How did she know our names?"

The woman behind the counter shrugs and walks away.

I Was Hungry

Aron looks into the cup Selanya has handed him. He has a lot of suspicion about tea since this whole thing started.

"So this is a magic potion?"

Selanya answers calmly, but on the inside is rolling her eyes and making an exasperated sigh. "No, just an herbal tea, Aron. It should help you relax and focus."

Raising his eyebrows, Aron asks, "Natural herb?"

"Not that herb. Just store-bought herbal tea."

Aron grins, "I hear that herb helps you relax. So I hear."

Selanya rolls her eyes. "But that herb does not help you

focus. So focus. Tell me everything you can remember. Start with what you lost yesterday."

"Lost what?"

"Time. The time you lost most recently."

With another internal eye roll, Selanya thinks he may have had some of that natural herb before getting here today.

"I don't remember much. I was in the living room. Jack was talking, and then I was walking across the bridge downtown."

"Do you remember what you were thinking or feeling the minute you were on the bridge?"

Aron squints and tighten his lips but says nothing.

"Don't think about it, just answer as fast as you can. What's the very first thing when you were suddenly on the bridge?"

"I was thinking I was hungry, and tired."

"Why were you tired?"

In a matter-of-fact tone, Aron says, "I had just climbed up from the riverbank."

Aron is a little disturbed by what he just said. He had forgotten that. Forgotten the climb. Forgotten being wet. Forgotten slipping on the bank into the water.

"Why was I climbing up from the riverbank?

"Exactly. Why *were* you climbing up from the riverbank?"

He responds quickly, "Because I was chasing the rabbit."

Aron is even more disturbed by that statement. That's

really not normal. Chasing rabbits. But he remembers it now. It's all coming back quickly.

"Why was I chasing a rabbit? Because I was hungry. What am I saying?"

"It's okay. You're remembering. I think we're getting somewhere."

"Somewhere really creepy."

She pauses before she asks, "Did you eat the rabbit?"

Standing up, he shouts, "No!"

Selanya uses a calm voice to try to reel him back in before he freaks out too much.

"See, it's not that creepy. You didn't eat the rabbit."

"No. No, I didn't eat the rabbit. Because curry sounded better."

Selanya stares at Aron with a furrowed brow.

He explains, "Jenna was bringing home curry for dinner. I didn't want to fill up on rabbit when I was having curry later."

"Okay. See, this isn't creepy. Even when you were chasing the rabbit, you were reasoning. You were in control. Somewhat."

Aron sits and starts calmly working through this new realization, but he becomes more and more freaked out as he thinks about it.

"Yes. In control, and hungry. Hungry for rabbit. But prefer curry. What if I get hungry tonight? We're going to the gallery tonight. What if the food isn't good? What if they don't have food? We're not going until seven! What if I get hungry at the gallery?"

"Calm down. we don't even know that getting hungry is the trigger."

Aron continues thinking about tonight's event, "Maybe they'll have rabbit on crackers. I don't think I even like rabbit."

Episode Eight

WRONG NUMBER

Reunion

A man holds the door for Marinette as she walks into the hotel lobby. She smiles to demonstrate her appreciation. He starts to speak, but just smiles back. The desk clerk eagerly greets her.

"Good afternoon, Ms. Sola."

"Hello, Alex. Glad to see your smiling face."

"Well, it's easy to smile when our guests are as friendly as you."

"You flatter me."

"There is a message for you."

Alex turns to retrieve an envelope from the counter behind her. Marinette wonders who even knows she is here, but she keeps her surprise from Alex.

"Here it is."

Alex hands her a square envelope with "Mari" written on the front.

"A very *interesting* man left it earlier."

She chose the word "interesting" very carefully, and with

intonation to leave it open to interpretation to mean weird, strange, or odd.

"Thank you. Have a good afternoon."

"And you too, Ms. Sola."

Marinette flips the envelope over as she walks toward the door to the patio. She immediately recognizes the wax seal with the letter S stamped into it. Just like him to play it so cloak and dagger. She opens the letter and pulls out an invitation card that simply reads "Your place or mine?"

She sighs. Then laughs, "I assume the choice is not mine."

"The choice is always yours."

She looks up from the note to see Shamus holding the patio door for her. She walks through the door as if she is ignoring him, but then grabs his hand as she passes and pulls him onto the patio.

"Good to see you, Shamus. Have a seat. Let's chat. How long has it been?"

"I lost count. Perhaps long enough for old grudges to have faded?"

She says defensively, "I was never one to hold a grudge."

Shamus fights back rolling his eyes, "No. You were more about revenge, I guess."

"And you? Old resentments linger?"

"I'm good. There was never resentment. Just disenchantment. Long time to think about it, a couple of decades maybe, while I was sitting in that little glass prison you conjured up for me. Decided to just let it go."

"Well, I did have something like a regret about that. I sent someone to get you out when I realized I might have been misinformed about your infidelity."

"Misinformed. Is that a synonym for wrong?"

She smiles. "You know I am never wrong."

"And you know I'll never believe that."

"So. To what do I owe this nice little visit, Shamus?"

"I wondered what could have possibly brought you all the way here from your beloved New Orleans."

"A girl likes to travel. I needed a little getaway."

"And you know I'll never believe that either."

"You obviously already know, Shamus. Don't be so dramatic."

"I know better than to ask who called you here. Some poor guy is about to find out what a woman scorned can really do, but why such an interest in Aron? He and Jenna are obviously in love. He would never cheat on her or be cruel to her."

She leans in and whispers, "He's one of mine."

"A skin-walker," Shamus clarifies, "but not one of your werewolves."

"I don't play favorites. I protect them all. And it would be easier to do if he were in New Orleans with me."

"There's more going on here than you know, Marinette."

"Witches? I know about them."

"Do you know about Jack?"

She pays attention. She realizes that Shamus really

doesn't know who called her. She's not going to tell him.

“I've heard the name. Never met him.”

“He's Aron's brother. A plain ol' human that for some reason has been pulled into our world. It started when a witch from the Hungarian lineage put a spell on Aron to try to manipulate Jack. And it went all wrong.”

Marinette realizes he is talking about Sunder. Still holding her cards close, her expression gives nothing away. Not even as she thinks about how annoying wish-granting fairies can be. She is having serious doubts about doing anything to help Sunder.

“More reason for me to protect Aron. More reason for him to come to New Orleans. He's my concern, not this Jack.”

“Are you sure? Jack is Aron's brother, and somehow ended up in the Sweet Shop.”

“You said he was mortal.”

“As far I or anyone else can tell, he is.”

“Is he a wizard, Catalin, Finn? He's not an angel is he? They can act just like mortal sometimes. So annoying.”

“No, I went through the whole list myself. He and Aron are both born mortal humans. But the universe, or someone, has thrown Jack into my plane of reality more than once. People don't get there by accident. I don't think you should interfere with the situation here. It could be dangerous.”

“And when have you known me to worry about *dangerous*, Shamus? I am the danger others fear.”

“I won't argue with that. But if you really want to protect

Aron, I don't think taking him away from here is the way to do it."

"And I don't think it's up to you."

"No. I can't tell you what to do. But before you decide, meet him yourself. Before you uproot Aron and Jenna from this place, take a good look and see if you can figure out what's going on. And if you can, please let me know. I really can't understand it myself."

Not like Shamus to admit he doesn't know the answer to a riddle. Marinette thinks maybe she should meet this mortal Jack. Or maybe not. She gets up, "It's been nice seeing you again, Shamus. Let's do this again in a couple hundred years."

"Call me anytime you need me, Mari."

"I will, Shamus. Like I said, in a couple hundred years."

He watches as she walks back into the lobby. She may be the only person that he ever lets have the last word. She is certainly the only one that ever leaves the room before him.

At Your Service

Sunder is studying a pink necklace that may go well with a new dress she bought. She holds it up to her neck and looks in a mirror on the counter. Marinette leans in, looking at it in the mirror also.

"That is very nice. This one would look much better on

you."

Marinette hands Sunder a necklace with black and blood red stones.

Trying not to show how startled she is that someone approached that closely without her noticing, Sunder takes the necklace and holds it up to her neck.

"That *is* beautiful."

"Let me help you."

Marinette helps Sunder with the clasp on the necklace. Sunder admires it in the mirror.

"How much is it?"

"I have no idea," Marinette responds.

"I'm sorry; I thought you worked here."

"No, I'm just shopping, too."

Sunder looks back at the mirror.

"Well, you have wonderful taste."

"Thank you."

Sunder takes the necklace off and places it back on the display. She notices the onyx necklace Marinette is wearing.

"I like your necklace. Very stylish. Where did you get it?"

"It's an old family heirloom. I've had it for a few hundred years or so."

Sunder looks at Marinette carefully. She feigns a smile at what she is considering may be a joke. Or an acknowledgment. She turns on her "charmed to meet you" voice and investigates.

"I know we haven't met, but you look so familiar."

"That's not surprising . . . Sunder."

"You know me?"

"Maybe better than you know yourself."

Sunder loses the fake charm.

"Who are you?"

"Who did you summon?"

Sunder is speechless.

"I'm Marinette. At your service. Or soon to be. Right now, I have to find someone else who needs to meet me. But I'll be back. Count on it."

Marinette turns to leave, but before she takes more than a couple of steps, she looks back at Sunder.

"I am so going to enjoy doing business with you, Sunder Bouchard."

The Touch Of An Artist

Aron is mainly thinking about the hors d'oeuvres as he and Jenna talk to Liam at the opening. But he tries to say something to show he is participating in the moment.

"Have you sold anything yet?"

"Two pieces," Liam brags.

"That's good?"

"Good enough to make this evening worth it. Be nice if I sell more, or people come back later to buy. But I am calling it a success."

Jenna, sounding like she just found a four-leaf clover, says, "There she is."

Aron and Liam ask, "Who?"

"The woman I met today. She's really interesting."

Jenna walks over to Marinette, leaving Aron and Liam to continue wondering who this new woman is.

Marinette reaches her hands out to greet Jenna. "I'm so glad you told me about this event. There are some wonderful works here."

"*I'm* so glad you made it."

Jenna motions for Aron and Liam to come over.

"I want you to meet the artist, and my fiancé."

"Nice to meet you," Liam says, "I'm The Artist." He rolls his hand and bows.

"And I, am The Fiancé," Aron adds mimicking Liam's bow.

Jenna rolls her eyes at the two of them.

"They have names. Liam, this is Marinette. And this is Aron. Marinette is visiting from . . . you know, I don't think I asked where you were from."

"Most recently from New Orleans."

"Oh, I love New Orleans," Jenna says.

Aron smile. "That's one of the places she was considering for our honeymoon."

Marinette looks into Aron's eyes for a moment before she says anything. "Of course. You must feel at home in New Orleans."

Aron and Jenna tilt their heads and look at each other. Marinette looks at Jenna, then back at Aron.

"It's a wonderful place for musicians," Marinette explains.

"I told her you were a musician," Jenna adds.

Aron nods with understanding, "Yeah, there's some cool places there to hear all kinds of music. I love that city."

"Yes. All kinds of music," Marinette says, "All kinds of people. And some of my favorite people are musicians." She winks at Aron.

He is confused, and relieved to see Jack walk into the room to give him a reason to disengage from the conversation, "There's Jack."

Jenna leans in close to Aron, "What is he doing here?'

"He's Liam's friend too, Jenna."

Liam and Aron excuse themselves and go to talk to Jack, leaving Marinette to talk to Jenna, "You're not fond of his brother?"

"I'm sorry. We just have a bit of a disagreement on what's in Aron's best interest."

Aron leaves Liam with Jack and comes back over to Jenna, "I hate to leave so soon, but I am getting a little hungry."

Jenna looks at Marinette, "There's a great place next door. Mari, you should join us."

“That's very kind of you. I'd like that.”

Aron, still a little uncomfortable with Marinette, “Yeh, it's really good. Prob'ly not as good as places in New Orleans.”

Marinette smile, “I am sure it will be delirious. But let me say my goodbyes to the artist.”

Marinette walks over to Liam and Jack who are laughing at something Jack just said.

“Apologies for interrupting. I just wanted to tell you how wonderful your exhibit is before I go. Maybe you'll have a showing in New Orleans soon.”

“Thank you so much. That would be wonderful.”

“And you must be Jack.”

“That depends on what you've heard,” Jack reaches out his hand to Marinette. She takes it with one hand and clasps it with the other.

'Marinette,” she says as she looks him in the eye.

Jack feels a cold pain creeping from his finger tips toward his arm. It was that feeling he remembers well. The stone cold paralysis. And another feeling, like a pin stabbing the back of his hand. He looks at his hand as she releases it. It looks normal. He quickly regains his composure, “Very nice to meet you.”

“And you. And what I have heard is that you are Aron's brother.”

“I've learned to answer to that,” Jack smiles, “He has a lot of fans. Are you one of them?”

“I've only recently found out about him, but I am already

a fan," then to Liam, "I see great things in your future. It was nice to meet you both."

As she turns to go, Jack rubs his hand, trying to casually inspect it for signs of damage. He wonders if Stoneclad's power is still having an affect on him. He doesn't connect that feeling to Marinette. But she noticed his body's defensive reaction to her attempt to inject a little vengeance. Maybe Shamus was right. Maybe she doesn't want to be a part of whatever this situation is.

Fate

Selanya stoops down to look at the lower shelves of a short bookcase. When she stands up, Shamus is there.

"What mortal life are you meddling in now?"

"I'm not *meddling,* Shamus. I'm trying to help."

"You know he's a skin-walker."

"I know."

"What does he know?"

"That he gets hungry and chases rabbits. Not much more."

Shamus banters, "Doesn't know much more or chase much more than rabbits?"

"Either."

"This is what I have been trying to make you understand.

Sunder messed with a spell that was over her head, thinking she knew all about the legend, but paid no attention to the warnings in the legend. See what happens?"

"I know."

Shamus folds his arms. "Do you? Then why are you looking for a way to fix it?"

"Are you suggesting we just leave him as a shape-changer? It will drive him crazy."

"Maybe, or maybe he'll learn to like it . . . once he can control it."

She crosses her arms, mocking his earlier parental posture of disapproval.

"Once he can control it? Why can't you just tell me what you know?"

He smiles, "And what fun would that be?"

"For you, or me? You're the one always preaching fate; maybe he came to me for a reason."

"Ooh, point."

He walks over to the comfy chair and sits.

"For that matter, Shamus, maybe *Sunder* is the reason. Maybe she's the one we really need to help."

"Maybe. Doubt it. Still something about her I don't like. But she's not the biggest problem in town right now."

Selanya sits in a chair next to his.

"Spill it, Shamus."

"How much do you know about Vodou?"

I'm Here for You

Jenna, Aron, and Marinette have finished a meal at the restaurant next to the gallery.

"That was good," Aron says, "I was starved."

"I bet you were," Marinette says with a wink.

Aron folds his napkin and avoids further eye contact.

"You're a big healthy guy and those hors d'oeuvres at the galley weren't very filling."

"That's true."

"They didn't even have any duck or rabbit."

Aron is taken aback by the statement. Jenna just thinks it's odd. Or maybe it's the latest food fad.

She asks, "Would those be hors d'oeuvre in New Orleans?"

"If you make them sweet and spicy enough, they could be."

Jenna politely excuses herself for a minute, and leaves Marinette and Aron alone at the table.

"Does she know?"

Aron doesn't understand, "Know what?"

"That you're a skin-walker?"

"A what?"

Marinette didn't expect Jenna would know, but she had not considered that Aron didn't know himself.

She wonders how much he does know, "Are you

blacking out?"

Aron says nothing. He looks at Marinette while he tries to decide if he should answer or not.

"You are. That's quite normal in the beginning. Especially if there is no one there to explain to you what's happening."

She waits incase he wants to speak. He doesn't. She has her answer.

"You transform. Into another animal. I suspect a cat of some sort. I could see you as a panther."

Aron listens.

"There are many skin-walkers in New Orleans. Werewolves. Other animals. A raven or two. I protect them."

"That's what's happening to me?"

"Yes. It might sound frightening to you right now, but you'll learn to control it. And to embrace it. But you need someone to help you understand it. Why don't you come back to New Orleans with me so I can protect you?"

"I don't think Jenna would want to move to New Orleans."

"Let me make it clearer. You are coming back with me. Make whatever arrangements with Jenna you need. The next new moon you see will be in New Orleans."

Mama Told Me

The next morning, Marinette makes good on her promise to return to discuss business with Sunder. She shows up at Sunder's house not long after Sunder has woken, and before she has had her usual morning tea. Sunder starts with the required hostess offering of something to drink or some cookies, but Marinette takes a seat and gets right to business.

"Tell me about the man you seek to be free from."

"Actually, I want him to be free of the woman that is trying to steal him from me. I know he loves me, but she is planting ideas in Jack's head to turn him against me. Controlling him."

Marinette takes a deep breath and sighs. "You seek revenge."

"I think of it more as liberation."

Marinette looks around the room, studying the art and the books on display. Then she looks Sunder up and down.

"You don't seem like a Vodou priest. How did you learn to summon me?"

"My mother spent several years in New Orleans before I was born. She taught me many things she learned there. She had a lot of stories about Mama Oya, Papa Legba, and you. There were others, but the three of you seemed to be her favorites."

"Were we? And was your mother a vengeful woman like you?"

Sunder takes offense at that characterization, but one thing her mother taught her about Marinette was that you should never offend her, and never make her angry.

"Mother had a kinder way of looking at people. She was more trusting perhaps than myself. Talked about karma and such."

"Did she explain to you that when you summon me to release you from a bondage, I can also send you back to it when I wish?"

"She did."

Marinette sits back.

"Tell me about Jack, and his brother."

"Aron?"

"Tell me how he became a skinwalker." Marinette already knows, but wants to see just how deep a hole Sunder will dig for herself.

Sunder knows how dangerous Marinette can be, but also has extreme confidence in her own powers of persuasion.

"I think it was something Selanya did. I'm telling you, she is bad news for Jack, and Aron."

Marinette stands up and moves over next to Sunder. She looms over her with a threatening glare.

"Your request for my services is denied."

Sunder knows her mother said Marinette must be treated with the utmost respect, and hides her fear behind a disappointed face, "But why?"

"Your problems with Jack are not my concern. It seems you brought on Aron's condition and your own ill fate all by yourself. It was *not* Jack's doing. And it wasn't Selanya's doing."

Sunder's fear morphs into anger. She clenches her jaw to keep herself from lashing out at Marinette.

"I'm going to be taking Aron back to New Orleans. He's one of mine now, thanks to you. I do appreciate the gift. I'll be watching out for Aron. And any of those that belong to him. Since Jack is his brother, I will keep an eye on Jack too."

"That's very kind of you. Will watching out for Jack include keeping him safe from Selanya?"

"It will include keeping him safe from you, pixy. You're like those tiresome Vodou priests that take money and call me to bind someone with a blind love. But you aren't even as powerful as those bokors with their black magic. You're just a wish fairy from the frigid north."

As Marinette turns to walk away, Sunder feels every muscle in her body start to relax, after tensing up with the thought of what Marinette could do to her. But they tighten once again as Marinette stops and looks back.

"You should forget everything your mother taught you about calling on me. If I ever have to come back to deal with your silly little magic, Sunder, you will regret it."

Cold Feet

The front door opens. Aron stands at the threshold with no shoes. Jenna looks from the couch, not sure what to say.

"I can tell you anything. Right?"

She walks over to him, takes his hand, and pulls him into the room. She shuts the door, leads him to the couch, and sits next to him.

"You know you can."

Aron hopes that is true. He breathes deeply and gathers all his strength to speak.

"I've been blacking out. Like before. I wake up in places and I don't know how I got there."

He decides to leave out any parts about blood, or rabbit chasing. For now. Maybe forever. But she deserves to know something is happening, and that he is scared.

"Aron. I knew you were going through something. I'm glad you are talking about it now."

"I love you, Jenna."

"I love you, too. We can get through whatever this is together. We need to take you to a doctor. Maybe a neurologist."

"I don't think that will help."

"You're blacking out. You need medical help."

Aron gets up and looks out the window. Maybe the words he needs to say are out there. But no inspiration comes, so he just says what he thinks.

“I don't think it's medical. Please don't get mad, but I think it has something to do with what Sunder did.”

He keeps looking out the window as he waits for her response, or for something she threw to hit him. But there is only silence. When he turns, she is gone.

“Jenna?”

He finds her in the kitchen. Crying.

“I'm sorry. I know you don't want to hear any of that stuff, but she did something to me, and I'm scared.”

“You don't want to get married, do you?”

“No, Jenna, I mean of course I do. I love you. I can't imagine my life without you.”

“Then why are you torturing me like this? Blaming the way you have been acting on witches. Did you even have amnesia before?”

“Yes. I still don't remember where I was all that time. Or recently.”

“Is there someone else? Is that where you've been?”

“No. Jenna believe me. I love you. Only you. But I am scared. I am scared I have been turned into some sort of monster.”

Time to Go

With Sunder's foolish quest behind her, it's time for Marinette to take Aron home. As she approaches the house, Jenna storms out the front door.

"Jenna?"

Tear stains mar Jenna's face.

"Are you ok?" Marinette asks.

"I just had a fight with Aron. I had to get out."

"I'm so sorry. The two of you seem so happy together. What happened?"

Even though they only met recently, Jenna starts telling Marinette everything as if they have been best friends for years.

"He says he's blacking out. I think he's just backing out, trying to make me leave him so he doesn't have to be the one to end it."

"He didn't strike me as being clever enough to think up something that complex."

Jenna smiles. "He's got his own kind of smarts, but you're right. He's not the kind to think up something so mean."

Aron comes out of the house, apologies on his lips. "Jenna, I'm sorry. I didn't mean to upset you."

He stops when he sees Marinette. He knows why she is there.

"It's okay, Aron. Jenna was just telling me how you would never do anything to hurt her on purpose."

“I wouldn't.”

“She's just worried about your blackouts.”

Marinette looks at Jenna who takes the cue.

“I am. I just got scared I was losing you.”

“You'll never lose me.” He holds Jenna, but he looks at Marinette. “I'm not going anywhere.”

Marinette smiles at him. She usually has little compassion for mortals, but these two were almost torn apart by a wish fairy. And she really has no compassion for witch fairies.

“No, I don't believe you are, Aron. I know the two of you will work this out. But I am going somewhere. I'm headed home to New Orleans today.”

Aron understands what she is telling him, and is relieved there isn't going to be a problem with Marinette, and that she didn't say anything about witches to Jenna.

“I just wanted to say goodbye first, and to tell you both that you're welcome to visit me in New Orleans anytime. On your honeymoon perhaps.”

Jenna collects her emotions.

“Thank you. I'm so glad we met you while you were here. And thanks again for coming to the art opening.”

“I enjoyed that, then looking at Aron, “It always nice to discover a new talent”

Jenna hugs Marinette then teary eyed heads into the house. Before Aron goes in, Marinette stops him.

“Aron, let me give you my number so you can call when you visit New Orleans.”

He makes sure Jenna is in the house before he speaks.

“Thank you. I could never leave her.”

“I know. I see that now.”

“Will I ever be normal again?”

“I hope not. Normal is very dull. I think you'll always have your gift. But you'll learn to control it. You'll learn to change only when you want to.”

“I don't think I'll want to.”

“Oh, you will. Take this.”

She hands him an onyx stone with a spiral rune etched into it.

“Carry this with you. Think of it as my direct line. Hold it tight in your palm and think of me. I *will* find you. Remember, I'm your protector.”

“Thank you.”

“One more thing. This brother of yours. His name keeps popping up everywhere. Jack has somehow found a way into a dangerous world where mortals don't belong, and I imagine there are a lot of occupants of that world that are not happy he has access. You may need to be his protector at some point. Tell him Shamus may act obtuse at times, but he should trust Shamus's insight. I do. He may be Jack's most powerful ally.”

“Shamus?”

“He'll know who you mean.”

The Legends Behind Witches

Seven Ravens

Witches and Legends One: A Bad Spell is based on several versions of a similar legend. Sunder uses a spell called Blackened Swan from her mother's cook book. This is based on the variations of ***The Seven Ravens,*** a German fairy tale collected by the Brothers Grimm. In The Seven Ravens, brothers were turned into birds. Other variations include *The Six Swans*, *The Twelve Wild Ducks*, *Udea and her Seven Brothers*, *The Wild Swans*, *The Twelve Brothers*, and *The Magic Swan Geese*.

A peasant had seven sons and one daughter. She was sickly. He sent his sons to get water for her, or to be baptized in the German version. In the Greek version, the water came from a healing spring. The brothers rushed and dropped the jug in the well. When they did not return, their father thought they had gone to play instead of fetching the water, and he cursed them. Unintentionally, he turned them into ravens.

When the sister was grown, she searched for her brothers. She asks for help from the sun, the moon, and the morning star. The morning star gives her a chicken bone (in the Italian) or a bat's foot (in the Greek) and tells her she will need it to save her brothers. She finds the Glass Mountain where they are. In the Greek, she opens it with the bat's foot; in the German, she has lost the bone, and chops off a finger to use as a key. Inside the mountain, a dwarf tells her that her brothers will return. She eats the brothers' food and drink, and leaves a ring from home in the last cup.

When her brothers return, she hides, and they turn into human form and ask who has been at their food. The last one finds the ring, and hopes it is their sister, in which case they are saved. She emerges, and they return home. In the Six Swans version, one of the brothers returns with a wing instead of an arm.

Wizard Stone Clad

An internet search for the word **Adawehi** (Ah-dah-way-hee) in the Cherokee language returns several meanings: the spirit of healing, water conjurer, medicine man, magician, conjurer witch.

One of the Adawehi of legends is called Stoneclad or Nûñ'yunu'wï, which means "dressed in stone" or "Stone Clad". He was an ancient ada'wehi that preyed on the Cherokee. Then later, before they killed him, he gave them many of their traditional medicines and ceremonies.

The stories of Stoneclad vary from one telling to another. In some versions there is only one. In others there is a race of Stoneclads. Stoneclad can be a man-sized human witch that turned himself into an invulnerable monster. Or he can be a stone-skinned giant. Always, he has rock armor that protect him from weapons, fire, and cold.

In the Creek account the monster is stone-covered and his only vulnerable spot is in his ear. This myth has variations at other places in North America. The monster may be clad with stone, scales, or metal. Or may be only magically invulnerable. The vulnerable spot may be located in the foot, nose, ear. He can only be defeated through draining his power. This may be achieved by destroying his talismans or exposing him to menstruating women.

Marinette-Bwa-Chech

Marinette-Bwa-Chech is a loa in Haitian Vodou. It is believed that Marinette was burned alive for fighting against slavery and for the Bois Caiman ceremony that began the Haitian revolution. She relates to the horrible conditions that slaves had to endure. She is often considered to be angry loa, used in black magic. She is feared and acts upon those she possesses violently. The screeching owl is the emblem of Marinette. When she possesses someone they behave as an owl, hooking their fingers, lowering their heads and scratching. But she can also be seen as one who frees her people from bondage. Marinette is not cruel.

She is called up by the *bokor* (pronounce baw-kaw) who are priests and priestesses who work black magic. The ones who would be consulted to have an enemy killed, raise the dead necromancy, or bind someone in blind love. They will call upon Marinette. She has been known to be invoked for revenge against cheating boyfriends and husbands. Many say she should never be invoked because she is too dangerous and hostile. She is not a spirit for a Vodou novice like Sunder, no matter how self confident. In fact, Marinette can immediately identify a novice.

Marinette should never be invoked within the home because she literally burns with rage and may burn down buildings while within them, intentionally or not.

Marinette is the matron of werewolves and loups-garoux. She protects them. She is respected by werewolves, and some hold services in her honor. She likes salvia, black pepper, lavender, and sweets. Her *colors* are black and deep blood red. She is a bitter spirit who prefers to be alone. People disappointed her.

ABOUT THE AUTHOR

J. Smith Kirkland grew up in a 'haunted' house in Dallas Bay, Tennessee watching *Dark Shadows & The Outer Limits* – a spooky upbringing which explains why his stories tend to include ghosts, witches, folklore, and twisted plots and characters.

After obtaining degrees in Art and in Computers, and working for years in the computer industry, fate landed him in a role in the bizarre and bloody underground camp classic *Zombeak! w*hich stars a satan-possessed zombie-creating chicken. The experience opened a whole new world for him – one where he could share his own twisted tales by producing his own indie movies.

His indie works include *Witches*, a soap-opera-style web series which was shot in Dallas Bay and Chattanooga, Tennessee. The storylines in *Witches* are built around characters from the folklore of witches and Vodou. This Witches And Legends series was born from that web series.

Titles by J. Smith Kirkland

Non Fiction

- Growing Up Without WiFi

Fiction

- Witches and Legends Series
  - One: “A Bad Spell”
  - Two: “Curses and Cures”
  - Three: “Ghost Stories”
  - Four: “Dangers Of Magic”
- Skywords : The Incomplete Works Of J. Smith Kirkland
  - Contributions to the Crazy Buffet Club Collections 2017 thru 2025
- Tales of the Catalin Series
  - True Love
  - Spider
- Witch Ball
- Witching Hour

www.ingramcontent.com/pod-product-compliance
Lightning Source LLC
LaVergne TN
LVHW050325160826
845677LV00014B/3542

* 9 7 9 8 9 9 4 5 0 9 6 2 3 *